CRAVED

WOLVES OF THE RISING SUN #4

KENZIE COX

Published by Bayou Moon Press, LLC, 2015.

This is a work of fiction. Similarities to real people, places, or events are entirely coincidental.

Craved: WOLVES OF THE RISING SUN #4
First edition.

Copyright © 2015 Kenzie Cox.
Written by Kenzie Cox.

Join the Packs of the Mating Season

The mating moon is rising...

Wherever that silver light touches, lone male werewolves are seized by the urge to find their mates. Join these six packs of growly alpha males (with six-packs!) as they seek out the smart, sassy women who are strong enough to claim them forever.

The "Mating Season" werewolf shifter novellas are brought to you by six authors following the adventures of six different packs. Each novella is the story of a mated pair (or trio!) with their Happily Ever After. Enjoy the run!

Learn more at thematingseason.com

CRAVED: WOLVES OF THE RISING SUN

What happens in the bayou, stays in the bayou…

Devon Michelson is a man with a past. One he's worked hard to bury. But when the one woman he's always loved walks back into his life, suddenly he's willing to put everything on the line…including his freedom.

Five years ago, Scarlett Jacobs left everything behind in order to start a new life. But when someone close to her is murdered and her life is threatened, she's forced to go on the run. Again. And right back into the arms of the one man she never thought she'd see again—Devon Michelson.

Sign up for Kenzie's newsletter here at www.kenziecox.com. Do you prefer text messages? Sign up for text alerts! Just text SHIFTERSROCK to 24587 to register.

CHAPTER 1

DEVON

A Turbo Dog slammed down on the bar in front of me and was followed by an impatient sigh.

I glanced over at my sister Arianna. "What's with the heavy breathing? Were you and Luc making out in the stock room again?"

"Very funny." She rolled her eyes. "Dude, put that damned phone away. Do you ever stop working? There are at least half a dozen girls over at that table competing for the honor of warming your bed tonight." She plopped down on the stool beside me. It was Friday night and we were currently hanging out in the bar her mate co-owned with his brothers.

"Not my type." I glanced once more at the surveillance app on my phone and then closed it, satisfied everything was quiet. Two weeks ago, after the Riveauxs found an illegal grow site on one of their bayou islands, I'd been hired to set up surveillance and monitor every square inch of their property. So far there'd been no activity.

Arianna raised a skeptical eyebrow. "Not even the one sitting by herself over in that booth?"

I cast a quick glance across the room at the raven-haired beauty poring over a stack of paperwork. A slow smile pulled at my lips. Now that one… she had potential. Just the type of challenge I needed after a long week of office bullshit.

Arianna laughed. "You always did like making things hard on yourself."

I smirked. "Life's more interesting that way."

"Or just more exhausting."

I gave her a side-eye glance. Her normally wavy dark hair was tied up into a sleek ponytail, and the sundress she wore showed off her flawless bronzed skin. She looked exactly the same as she always did with one notable exception—the pure joy shining in her dark eyes. I wasn't used to seeing that, and a twinge of jealousy made my chest tighten. Had I ever felt that way?

Once maybe, for about half a second right before my life went to shit again.

"Nah, little sis." I glanced over her head and nodded at her mate, Luc. "Not all of us can be so lucky in the love department. I might as well have some fun with it, right?"

She shook her head. "Whatever you say, Dev."

I narrowed my eyes at her, irritated. "You know how I feel about that name."

"Crap." She grimaced. "Sorry. It just slipped out."

"Don't worry about it." I grabbed my beer and stood, needing some space, something to distract me from my past threatening to crash through my defenses. Pocketing my phone, I strode across the bar, straight toward the one woman in the room who had yet to even look in my direction.

When I reached her table, she was pitched

forward, studying a document, her long dark hair obscuring most of her face.

"Excuse me," I said, eyeing her incredibly long legs from her stiletto heels all the way up to the hemline of her short skirt.

"Not interested," she said without even looking my way.

I grinned. Perfect. "How can you tell?"

Her shoulders stiffened, but otherwise she ignored me.

"At least let me buy you a drink."

"Thanks, but I'm meeting someone."

"All right. But don't hesitate to let me know if you change your mind."

Nothing. Total silence. Not even a glance in my direction.

Damn. Major shutdown. Shaking my head, I retreated back to the bar.

"What's this? Did I really just watch you completely strike out?" Amusement danced in Arianna's eyes. "Unbelievable."

"Enjoy it while you can, Ari, 'cause it's only the top of the first inning. The game's far from over."

"*Right*." She leaned into her mate, Luc.

He pulled her in closer, nuzzling her neck as he ran his fingers lightly down her bare arm. The moment was so naturally intimate I felt like I was intruding and had to look away.

Intimacy. Not really my thing.

Computers. Data. Code. That was where I was most comfortable. My fingers itched for my keyboard. There were only two ways to curb the unease starting to grip me. Hot sex or an all-nighter fighting firewalls. I glanced once again across the room at the dark-haired woman.

Silas, the Riveaux brothers' cousin, was standing in front of her table, his hands shoved in his pockets, staring down at her with piqued interest. He wore a black T-shirt, jeans, and work boots. Vibrant tattoos covered both arms. I'd just met the guy a few hours ago, but there was a roughness about him that said he was no stranger to trouble.

I sat back and waited for her to give him the same brush-off she'd given me.

Only she didn't.

She lifted her head, and then after a second, she waved a hand indicating he should sit down.

What the—?

"Hey, Luc." Rayna, the bartender and one of Luc's pack, hastily set two beers on the table. "Make yourself useful and take these drinks over to Silas."

Luc scowled, but before he could respond she took off in the other direction.

"I'll do it." Not waiting for an answer, I grabbed the drinks and headed over to Silas and the one girl I was determined to talk to.

With her hair now tucked behind one ear, I got my first full glimpse of her face and felt the air rush out of my lungs.

Scarlett?

It couldn't be. Not here. Not now.

I forced one foot in front of the other, unease and excitement warring for dominance. If it was her… I swallowed, unable to tear my gaze from her intense blue eyes and the way she was studying Silas. Son of a… If they had something going, I was going to lose my fucking mind.

My heart started to pound against my rib cage, and my fingers tightened around the bottles I held.

Maybe it wasn't her. This version had dark hair instead of light and a slightly curvier body. But her face… and holy Christ. The tattoo.

How had I not noticed it before? The intricate vine anklet around her left foot was the exact same one I'd worked into the edges of the broken heart that was inked on my left shoulder.

It was her.

The only girl I'd ever loved.

The one I hadn't seen in over five years. The one who still haunted my dreams.

CHAPTER 2
SCARLETT

Silas Davenne was trouble. The quintessential bad boy with the attitude to match. Tall, muscular, brooding. The type most women couldn't help drooling over.

But not me. I was here on business. The life-and-death kind.

And Silas Davenne was my only hope. Clutching the file I'd found only four days ago, I sucked in a breath and steeled myself. It was now or never.

"Scarlett?"

At the sound of my name, I jerked my head up and let out a tiny, startled gasp. My ex-boyfriend Devon Mickelson loomed over the table with two beers in his hands.

An all-too-familiar bolt of excitement shot through me, followed quickly by a large dose of ice-cold reality. No. He couldn't be here in this tiny little bayou town. Not now. He was from my past. A past I'd buried years ago. One that had to stay that way. For all our sakes.

My throat went dry and my mouth worked before I was finally able to force out, "Devon?"

"I go by Smoke now." He placed the beer on the table, his dark gray eyes drinking me in, searing me with their intensity.

A whisper of that long-suppressed craving he'd always managed to ignite filtered through me, and I felt my wolf scratch at the surface.

No! This couldn't happen. Not now. Not ever again.

I tore my gaze from him and met Silas's curious stare. I cleared my throat. "Um, Silas, this is Dev—"

"Smoke," my ex said. "And Silas and I already know each other."

"You do?" I glanced between the two of them, unease making my shoulders tense. Shit! Now what? I'd made the trip to southeast Louisiana from Nashville because I needed help. Not so I could be dragged back into a life full of shady dealings and questionable contacts. There was a reason I'd left Devon five years ago and hadn't looked back.

Before either could answer, I stood. "I shouldn't have come here. I'm sorry to waste your time, Mr. Davenne. But I think I'd better be going."

With my heart hammering, I clutched the file tight to my chest, blinked back tears of frustration, and headed straight for the door.

"Wait." A large hand caught my wrist, stopping me. A hand I knew almost as well as my own.

"Let me go, Devon," I said without looking at him.

"Not until I get answers." His grip on my wrist was light, but there was no mistaking the demand in his tone.

I slowly turned toward him and stared at his hand still holding me in place. "Is this what you want? To force me to stay here and talk to you?"

It was a shitty thing to say, but I had to get out of there. Had to leave before I threw myself in his arms and never left.

He released me and let out a small, frustrated sigh. "No, Scarlett. Dammit, that's not at all what I want. But considering our history, don't you think you at least owe me a conversation?"

Pain and anger mixed in his tone, and I closed my eyes as if that would help me shove my guilt aside. "There's nothing to say."

"The hell there isn't."

We stood in the middle of the bayou bar, chatter and music filling the dead air between us. My chest tightened, and although the urge to flee was right there at the surface, my feet felt cemented to the wood floor. It had taken every ounce of strength I had to leave him that summer. And now that he was standing in front of me, it was as if no time had passed. He was the same—tattooed, intense, and full of so much passion he took my breath away.

"Devon, I—"

"It's Smoke," he barked, anger flashing through his haunted eyes.

"Sorry," I mumbled and reached out to touch his hand, but stopped suddenly and forced my arm to my side. His gaze tracked my movement, and heat crawled up my neck. What was I doing?

"Fuck." Frowning, he ran a hand through his already mussed hair.

"Excuse me," Silas said, coming up behind Devon. "Sorry to interrupt this, ah… interesting reunion, but we still have business to discuss."

I shook my head and opened my mouth to protest again, but Silas cut me off.

"Enough. Bax sent you to me for a reason.

I'd be dishonoring my word to him if I let you go now." He jerked his head toward the back of the bar. "Let's take this somewhere more private." Eyeing Devon, he added, "If you have time, I'd like you to sit in on this meeting."

I opened my mouth to protest, but Devon nodded and asked, "Who's Bax?"

Crap.

"He was her mate."

I sucked in a sharp breath and met Silas's gaze. "He knows about… us?"

"Yes, I know," Devon all but growled as if he were a wolf himself. Only I already knew he wasn't. I'd have picked up on his scent.

"His sister is with my cousin, Luc," Silas said. "Don't worry. He's trustworthy."

The hell he was. Devon Michelson—Smoke—had a code name for a reason.

"You said *was* her mate," Devon said to Silas, his tone neutral, as if he were merely curious. "What happened?"

"Bax was recruited by the FBI shortly after he left the Marines. Two years ago he was killed on the job."

I was numb. There were no tears. No gut-wrenching heartache. No sucker punch to the gut at the mention of Bax's death. Not anymore. My mate's death was almost surreal now, like the year we'd had together never actually happened. It had gotten easier to forget, to put that time behind me. Or had been until I'd found the death threat in my mailbox.

"She's been turned then," Devon said to himself as if he was just realizing the implications of what Silas had revealed about me.

His words made me feel more exposed than

if I'd been stark-naked in the middle of the bar. Wrapping my arms around myself, I glanced around nervously, my skin itching and every fiber of my being screaming to shift.

To run. To find a safe place away from everyone.

Only I knew no such place existed. Not since I'd found out they were watching me. My only hope was Silas.

I turned my back on Devon and moved toward Silas. "You said something about going somewhere more private?"

"This way." The large ex-marine gestured for us to follow and led us into an empty office at the back of the bar. Silas sat behind the large banker's desk and waved for us to take a seat. "This is Luc's office. He's graciously let us borrow it for this meeting."

I sat in one of the armchairs, pointedly ignoring Devon.

Except even though I wasn't looking at him, I could smell the faint trace of his light, woodsy scent. And all the memories came rushing back: the pair of us cutting school while we made out in the back of his pickup truck, waking up next to him after sneaking out of my foster parents' house, slow dancing with him at the club no one should've ever let us into.

Dammit, Scarlett. Snap out of it.

I shook my head, trying to dislodge the image of him smiling down at me, the promise of our future still shining in his too-bright eyes.

Silas cleared his throat and cast his gaze on Devon. "I want it understood that everything you hear tonight is confidential. No one learns about this unless and until we're ready to talk, got it?"

Devon leaned forward, a small crease in his brow. "You know my people won't like that."

I curled my hands into tight fists. *His people.* Nothing ever changed. Still shady. Still dangerous. This had been a bad idea.

"That can't be helped," Silas said. "We don't know who can be trusted. So for now, us three, my two brothers, and the Riveauxs are the only ones who know anything. Got it?"

"Sure, man." Devon sat back, stretched his legs out in front of him and crossed his arms over his chest. "You need me to hack something?"

The obvious pleasure in his tone turned my heart to stone. He'd always loved his computers more than he had anything else. Including me. All the anger I'd harbored, had buried, had told myself was gone, came rushing back. But instead of turning to fiery passion like it once had, all I felt was cold, hard, and unforgiving. "Why else would he need you?"

Devon's entire body tensed as he turned his narrowed gray eyes on me, anger and something beyond danger flashing in them. The muscles in his forearms flexed, and a small vibration ran through him before he slowly sat back, forcing himself to appear relaxed. Only it didn't take a wolf to know he was coiled and ready to strike. That was clear by the nonstop tapping of two fingers on the back of his phone. "It's like that, is it?"

I steeled myself and didn't shy away from the storm brewing within him. He had to know where I stood. "Yeah. It's like that."

CHAPTER 3

DEVON

Her words sliced through me, tearing open the old wound that lay festering deep inside me. She was the one person in the world who knew what my old man's words did to me. The words he'd said just before he sold me to the foster family and then took off for good to no doubt gamble the money away or spend it on hookers.

I gritted my teeth and swallowed the harsh words poised on my tongue. She'd obviously been deliberately trying to piss me off. And she'd succeeded. But I'd be damned if I let her know it.

Completely ignoring her, I planted my feet on the floor and leaned toward Silas. "What kind of job are we talking about here?"

"It depends." He cut his gaze to Scarlett. "Did you bring Bax's computer?"

"No. It appears to have disappeared. I have to assume it was stolen by whoever left me this." She slid the folder she'd been clutching across the desk. "I found it earlier this week while I was packing up the last of Bax's things."

An image of her living with another man flashed in my mind, and I gritted my teeth against the scowl trying to break free. Dammit. She'd been mated. I'd seen my sister with Luc. There was no denying what that meant. Long ago, I'd resigned myself to the fact that Scarlett would never be mine again, but now I knew she never really had been.

The realization gutted me.

Silas took the file but didn't open it. "Who else knows about this?"

"Just me and his partner." There was a tremor in her voice that had me twitching to soothe her.

Fuck. I had to get the hell out of there. I stood. "You don't need me for this. After you're done here, brief me on the work and I'll get you whatever you need."

"Wait." Silas held his hand up and then stood, looming over the desk. "It's not an accident you're here for this conversation."

I raised one eyebrow. "How's that? I don't remember being asked to be at the bar for this meeting."

He chuckled. "That was fortuitous, wasn't it? But then Scarlett here *is* hard to resist. I definitely see why Bax chose her."

My fingers flexed involuntarily. "Get on with it, Silas."

"Of course." He sat back down. "I asked Luc to make sure you were at the bar because after I spoke with Scarlett earlier today, I was certain we'd need your services. But now that it's clear you two know each other, I have another favor to ask."

"What's that?"

Silas flipped the file open, glanced at the sheet inside, and nodded solemnly as if he was confirming something. Sweeping his gaze over Scarlett, his lips formed a thin line. "She can't go home. It's too dangerous. Whoever killed Bax is after her, and I have every reason to believe they could be working for the government."

"That's why I'm here," Scarlett said. "Bax told me you're the only one I could trust if everything went south."

"Right. But you can't stay with me. It's only a matter of days before they start looking for you here if they haven't already. Bax and I were in the same platoon. We have history." Silas waved a hand toward me. "But this one… he's completely under the radar. No one knows where he lives. I know for a fact he has at least four fake identities and am certain he has a dozen more. His code name's Smoke because he can penetrate just about any system he wants to, slither into any situation, and then he's gone, just like that."

Scarlett's eyes went wide with shock as she

stared at Silas. "You want me to stay with him?"

Something primal inside me screamed yes while my head was yelling fuck no. I couldn't be around Scarlett and not lose myself to her. That much was clear, no matter how many defensive walls I erected. She had a piece of my soul. And if she took any more, I'd never recover.

"Yes. It's the safest place for you," Silas said.

"I don't think—" I started.

"No!" Scarlett cut me off. "Never going to happen. I'll go somewhere else. I'll get on a bus and move across the country. Change my name. My hair. My style. Whatever. But I'm not staying with Devon."

Her horrified tone irritated me straight to my core. I turned to her. "Have you lost your mind? Are you seriously saying you'd rather take your chances running from the Feds than be subjected to staying in my guest room?"

"Like you have a guest room," she muttered and crossed her arms over her chest, her chin sticking out.

"Jesus, Scarlett. Grow up. We're not teenagers anymore." Her petulant attitude both irritated the fuck out of me and tugged at that tender place in my heart that had always been reserved for her. How many times had I seen her pouting just like that when she didn't get her way? And how many times had I teased my way past her defenses until she was laughing and falling into my waiting arms. All except for that last time. The one time she'd walked out on me and had never come back.

Silas shook his head. "You two can work this fight out on your own time. Right now we have more important things to discuss."

"Fine by me." I took a seat, determined to prove something not only to Scarlett but to myself. I would take her back to my house, and this time I'd do everything in my power to protect her or die trying. Silas was right. I had the tools and the experience to not only find any information they'd need but to keep her safe from outsiders.

"There's nothing to fight about," Scarlett said.

I snorted out a humorless laugh. "Whatever you say, sweetheart."

CHAPTER 4
SCARLETT

DEVON JERKED THE wheel of the white Ford truck, hugging the curve of the bayou road. He hadn't said a word to me once we'd left Silas in the bar known as the Wolves of the Rising Sun.

I couldn't exactly blame him though. I'd been so busy protecting myself from all the emotions trying to swallow me whole, I'd been a first-class bitch with my snide comments. Not to mention he had every reason to hate me after I'd left without even one word of explanation or a good-bye all those years ago. Yet here he was, going out of his way to protect me. Taking me back to his house, the one place that was his secret sanctuary. So secret that he'd told me Arianna didn't even know the location.

If he'd been anyone else, I might've been wary about his motives. But not Devon. He had his faults, but at his very core, he was good. It was what had drawn me to him and why I'd stayed for so long even when I knew I couldn't live his lifestyle. Couldn't be constantly looking over my shoulder, always on the run.

The irony of my current situation was not lost on me. And there was more than a small part of me that was relieved to be with him. He knew how to cover his tracks. No one would find me as long as I was with him.

"Thank you," I said quietly.

Devon took another turn. "What was that?"

I cleared my throat. "I said thank you."

"That's what I thought." The truck barreled down a two-lane bayou road, nothing in sight except creepy old tree canopies.

I gripped the passenger door, hanging on as he sped up. "That's all you have to say?"

"It is for now." His words were clipped and full of hostility.

I let out a sigh and stared straight ahead into the darkness. He had every right to hate me. I would if he'd done to me what I'd done to him. The only thing to do was wait him out. "When you're ready to ask your questions, I'll do my best to answer."

The truck slowed for a fraction of a second as he glanced over at me. But when I turned my head to look at him, he laid into the gas and the truck shot forward. "After we get home."

Home. As if we shared a place like we'd always planned. A pang of regret shot through my chest. Is this where we'd have lived if we'd followed through with our plans? Would we have moved to southeast Louisiana and been friends with wolves? I very much doubted it. I'd still be human and we'd either still be in Baton Rouge or behind bars.

But he was free. Had managed to stay out of jail and become someone the wolves trusted. Bax had trusted the Davennes, and he was the most aboveboard man I'd ever known. It's what had gotten him killed in the end. I knew that deep in my gut. He'd had information and someone had silenced him. Just like they were trying to silence me. Except I didn't know anything. They only thought I did.

Devon took what seemed like the thousandth turn and we finally pulled to a stop in front of a modest but well-kept two-story, wood-sided cottage.

"This is your place?" I asked, cringing at the surprised tone in my voice.

He glanced over at me, irritation flickering in his steely gaze. "Yes, Scarlett. I own it. Outright. I'm not a squatter, if that's what you're thinking."

"Uh, no. That's not what I was thinking at all." Son of a… I needed to get a handle on myself if I didn't want to insult him every five minutes for the next however many days. "It's nice."

He turned the truck off and just sat there for a moment. Then he opened the door and said, "Thanks," as he climbed out.

I blew out a breath and reached for the door handle, but before I could grab it, the door swung open and Devon stood on the other side, waiting.

"Still chivalrous, I see," I said and smiled at him.

"I never stopped."

My smile fell, and after grabbing my small duffle bag, Devon escorted me up the porch stairs and into the house. We were greeted by barking coming from the back of the house, followed by the patter of paws on his hardwood floors as a light-colored golden retriever barreled straight for me. I bent at the knee and met him eye to eye, holding my hand out as the goofy dog slobbered all over it. "This is your security system?"

"One piece of it." He cocked his head toward the wall and then strode straight over to an oversized alarm panel and entered at least two dozen numbers before the double beep sounded, indicating the alarm had been turned off. He glanced back at me. "And don't let him fool you. If an intruder tried to get in here, he'd likely take their leg off before they even got across the threshold."

"This guy?" I asked, scratching the dog behind his ears. "You've got to be joking."

"Fine, don't believe me. But if you break in, don't say I didn't warn you." His lips twitched into a small smile, and the ice encasing my heart started to melt.

"Got it. I'll take it under advisement."

His smile widened and I had to look away before I matched it. "Come on. I'll show you around." There was humor in his tone that told me he could see right through me.

Dammit. I hated that he could read me so well.

The dog stayed close to my leg as we headed into the airy living room. It was decorated with white walls, a forest-green couch, and green-striped armchairs. The entire back of the house was lined with floor-to-ceiling windows, giving the illusion of outdoor living.

"This is gorgeous," I said and then gave him a knowing smile. "You don't spend much time in here do you?"

He laughed. "No. As a matter of fact, I don't." And before I could ask where his office was, he strode across the room and opened a door. "Most days you can find me in here."

I crossed the room, anxiety rising up out of nowhere as I peeked into the cool, dark room.

A built-in desk lined two walls, complete with four monitors and enough equipment to build an international space station.

"I see nothing's changed," I said, stepping back into the living room.

Devon closed the door and leveled me with a fiery stare that could melt a glacier. "Everything has changed. You missed a lot in the past five years."

It was a look I'd never seen before. One full of righteous indignation. Not the slight guilt I was so used to when I chastised him for his illegal activity. I opened my mouth but closed it when I wasn't sure what I should say.

Devon sucked in a breath and shook his head. "Forget I said anything. It doesn't matter now. I'll show you to your room; then I have work to do."

He grabbed my duffle bag and took the stairs two at a time.

I glanced down at his dog. "It's going to be a long few days."

The golden retriever nudged my hand with his head and stared up at me with his bright brown eyes.

"You'll help me get through this, right?"

The dog sat, giving me his full attention.

"Thanks, buddy."

CHAPTER 5
DEVON

It was five minutes past six a.m., and I was just as wound up as I'd been five hours ago when I'd tried to get some sleep. The effort had been futile. All I'd done was lie in my bed thinking of Scarlett sleeping in the room next to mine. Unable to endure it any longer, I'd gotten dressed and headed straight for my office.

It wasn't the sanctuary I'd hoped it would be. The hum of my computers did little to settle my nerves. Nothing, not even breaking through the firewall and gaining access to Bax's ex-partner's computer, had calmed me down. All I could think about was the look on Scarlett's face when she saw my office.

The one that had disappointment written all over it.

Shit. I had to let that go. She was free to think whatever she wanted.

I sat back, waiting for the file transfer to finish. After I had everything safely stored in the cloud, I combed through the files for any mention of Bax or Scarlett.

I didn't have much to go on, just the information Silas had supplied. Bax had been killed while on an organized-crime case, and up until recently, Scarlett had been under the impression his death had happened in a shoot-out. Only the case was confidential and she'd never gotten any details.

But then an unaddressed, plain envelope had shown up on her desk four days ago. Inside was an incriminating document that implied someone in Bax's chain of command was engaged in human trafficking, and a short letter from Bax indicating that if she was getting this information, she was in danger and to leave town immediately. Strict instructions were left for her to contact Silas and to talk to no one else.

She hadn't been sure what to think since Bax had died two years earlier and life had gone on as normal. But then the following morning she'd come home to her apartment ransacked and a vague, threatening message written on her bathroom mirror. It had been enough to send her straight to Silas.

The documents left very little in the way of

clues, so I started working from the inside out. Bax's computer was no longer accessible. It had probably already been combed for information and wiped by now anyway. But his ex-partner, Fischer's, was still active. And if anyone had information on the days just before Bax's death, it was likely him. More often than not, foul play comes from those closest to us. I'd seen it dozens of times during my short tenure with the FBI.

A COMPLETED graphic flashed on my screen and I leaned forward, ready to run a massive search for Bax Carter through Fischer's files when a faint scream filtered through my closed door, followed by the unmistakable barking of my dog, Nate.

I was on my feet, my heart pounding against my ribs as I tore the door open and sprinted up the stairs toward Nate, who was now scratching at Scarlett's door, whining to get in.

"Nate!" I commanded. "Back up."

The dog stopped his scratching, but he didn't move. His body was tense and his eyes focused on the door. He wasn't going anywhere until he checked on her. "All right, buddy. I get it."

I swept past him and knocked once, not waiting for her response before I threw the door open.

Scarlett, clutching a pillow, let out a small gasp as she jerked back in surprise. Her dark hair had vanished, replaced by a pile of wavy blond locks she had piled on top of her head. Her real hair. Not the dark wig she'd used as a disguise.

"What happened?" I scanned the room on high alert for intruders as Nate leaped onto the bed, blocking her from my view.

"I'm sorry." Her voice was wobbly. "I had a nightmare."

I stopped peering out the window and turned toward her, the tension draining out of my shoulders. She was disheveled and gorgeous, sitting there in her tank top and pajama pants. "Nightmare?"

She nodded, petting Nate, who'd settled in next to her, his head resting on her leg. "They're always the same, but I haven't woken myself up from one in a while."

I blew out a breath. When I'd known her before, she'd never suffered from nightmares. When had they started? After her mate died? Without thinking, I sat on the bed next to her and automatically draped my arm over her shoulders, pulling her into me until her head rested on my chest.

Her body stiffened, and for a moment, I thought she was going to resist.

"Come on, Scarlett. No matter what happened between us, you're still my friend. I just want to help."

She let out a sad chuckle as I felt her relax into me. "Devon, we were never just friends."

"Fair enough. But I'd like to be one now if you'll let me." My words weren't exactly a lie. I did want to be there for her. Only it was obvious by the rush of heat claiming my body that I wanted so much more. I ached to trace the curve of her jawline, to kiss her pouty lips, to reacquaint myself with the long lines of her neck. To know her in every way possible.

Her fingers curled into my T-shirt as her breath hitched a little. "Okay."

That tiny word lit a beacon of hope inside my chest. *Friends.* As much as I'd tried to hate her for leaving, I couldn't. Deep in my heart I knew why she'd done it. And I couldn't blame her. She'd done what she had to. Just as I had.

I smiled down at her, and without any heat in my tone this time, I said, "The name's Smoke."

She shook her head. "Not to me it isn't."

My smile fell. "I'm not who I was back then, Scarlett."

She pulled away from me, her deep blue eyes still troubled. "Neither am I. But it doesn't change the fact that I'm always going to think of you as Devon. This code name, Smoke? All it does is make me think of the hacker in you. The part of you that I left. Can't you see that? If we're going to be friends, tap into whatever it is that brought us together before, then you're going to have to let me think of you as Devon. As that gangly teenager with his rough tattoos who had a heart of gold."

The fragile ball of hope fractured and shattered into a million pieces. My heart hardened, and I felt everything inside me shut down. She'd left the hacker. And that's all I was now.

I got up out of the bed and stood there with my hands buried deep in my jeans pockets. "It's fine. Call me whatever you want."

She was silent for a moment, then she said, "I'm sorry. I—"

"Forget it. I'll be downstairs if you need me. Working." Leaving Nate with her, I closed the door softly behind me and bit back a curse.

Everything I'd ever wanted was on the other side of the door. And I was everything she despised.

When I was halfway down the stairs, I heard her door creak open. "Devon?"

I paused but didn't look back. "Yes?"

"Can I use your shower?"

"Sure. There are clean towels in my bathroom. Help yourself."

"Thanks."

A few minutes later, I was back in my office when I heard the water rush through the old pipes. Images of her in the shower... naked... tormented me beyond distraction. Groaning, I pounded on the keyboard, taking my frustration out on the innocuous computer equipment.

CHAPTER 6
SCARLETT

THE NIGHTMARE WAS the same one I'd been having for the past three years, ever since the night I'd been turned werewolf. Me, alone in my Nashville apartment when a knock sounded on the door, followed by frantic screaming. It was my neighbor, Chelsea. She was in a panicked frenzy, half yelling and half crying about her boyfriend having been mauled by a large dog. And when I opened the door to let her in, she shifted right in front of me and then attacked, going straight for my throat.

Just thinking about that night makes me break out into a cold sweat. When the nightmares start, I can still feel the blood running down my chest as I lay there, bleeding out in my hallway.

I shuddered from the intense memories and flipped the water to scalding, wishing as I always did that the hot water could somehow finally strip away the horrors of that night.

It never worked, but the pain of the burning water did give me a sense of control. And by the time I stepped out of the shower, my skin was bright pink and a little tender. I stood in Devon's bathroom, unsure of what to do next. At home, I would've curled up on my couch with a bottle of wine and watched old chick flicks until I passed out. But I couldn't do that here.

Well, maybe I could. Minus the wine. Wine and Devon was a very bad idea.

I dressed quickly in a button-down shirt and my favorite jeans and then strode through Devon's room, careful to not look at his rumpled bed. When he'd been holding me in the guest room, I hadn't missed the faint sweet scent of his arousal. No matter what we said to each other, that attraction hadn't died between us and it likely never would.

Just a few days. That's what Silas had said. I could make it that long without throwing myself at him. But only if I got far away from his bedroom. In my hasty exit, I accidentally bumped into a side table he had next to the door, sending contents of his wallet scattering across the floor.

Dammit.

Kneeling, I grabbed a couple of business cards, his driver's license, and what appeared to be a credential of some sort. I flipped it over and let out a gasp of surprise.

FBI. Devon had a Federal Bureau of Investigation identification card.

How was that possible? He had a record. Not long after his eighteenth birthday he'd been caught up in a hacker bust and spent a week in jail. He'd gotten off with a stiff fine and a stern warning, but he still had a record. The FBI didn't hire anyone who couldn't pass a background check.

Was this for real? Was it possible he'd cleaned up his act and somehow made it into the bureau? Hope skated through me, but I shut it down just as fast. What if the ID was a fake? He'd made state IDs and driver's licenses before for his shitty foster parents as part of his "keep." It was either that or take his chances living on the streets. Was he still knee-deep in their bullshit? Or into something worse?

Nausea took over, and I hated that I still doubted him. Hated that my first impulse was to condemn the man I'd always loved even when I knew I couldn't be with him.

I studied the FBI ID one more time. If it was a fake, it was the best I'd ever seen. I shoved everything except the ID card into his wallet and then took off down the stairs, determined to get answers.

Bursting through his office door, I held the ID card up. "Where the hell did you get this?"

Devon stopped typing and swiveled around in his chair to stare at me. "Were you going through my wallet?"

"No. It fell on the floor. But that's beside the point. I need to know right now if this is for real, or if you're involved in something that requires you to impersonate an FBI agent. Because so help me, Devon, if I find out you're still messing around in the family business, I'll walk right out of this house and not look back. Threats be damned. I cannot be involved in anything like that. I won't."

His eyes widened at my accusation and then they narrowed in undisguised anger. He stood, his tall body uncurling like a snake ready to strike.

I took a step back, suddenly unsure of myself. While I'd basically just accused him of being in cahoots with his lowlife foster parents, the people I knew he'd hated, I didn't really believe it was possible. Not my Devon, the gentle guy who's only fault was that he liked to break into computers for money. What was I thinking?

"Let's get a few things straight here," he said, plucking the ID out of my hand. "Up until about two hours ago, I haven't broken the law in four years and twenty-two days. And this ID? It's an independent contractor's ID. I work for the FBI on my own terms. And if you really think I have anything to do with those assholes who used to call themselves my family, then maybe you should call Silas and let him know he needs to find you another safe house."

Shock held me stock-still as his words sank in. Of course he hadn't been involved with his foster family's illegal dealings. That was beyond a stupid thing to say. I knew better than anyone how much he hated them. That ID card had thrown me way off my game. "So… ah, you do work with the Feds?"

"Yes. And I don't need you coming in here and lecturing me while I'm risking not only my career but also my freedom in an attempt to help you." He stalked back over to his computer and pressed a key that made all his screens go dark.

Tears suddenly burned the backs of my eyes, but I angrily blinked them back. "Why?"

"Why what?"

"Why did you let me think you were a criminal? You must've known that's what I'd assume when I learned you were still hacking."

He threw his ID onto his desk and turned to me, his expression dark. "Because I am, Scarlett. I was when I struck my deal and I am today. I won't pretend to be something I'm not."

"But if you've been on the straight and narrow all this time…" He'd said he hadn't broken the law in years. There was no reason to not believe him. One thing Devon had never been was a liar.

"Don't you get it?" He stalked toward me, this time passion churning in his dark eyes. "I will always be that criminal. I will always crave the rush of finding my way past the most complicated security. If I wasn't working with the FBI, I'd still be illegally breaking into systems. I'd do it for money, for fun, for the challenge. It's who I am. Who I'll always be."

"No. It's not who you are," I said, my voice shaking. Four years and twenty-two days. He'd cleaned up before I'd even met Bax. If I'd known, I'd have come running back. Would've never been in this position. "You're channeling your skill into something better. You work for the FBI, for God's sake. You're one of the good guys."

"No! I'm not. Jesus, Scarlett. How can you be so naïve? Just because I'm doing work for the FBI doesn't make what I do any different. I break into networks, steal secrets, violate people's rights. Just because the government's paying me to do it doesn't make it legal. Hell, at least before I was able to control what information I let out. Now the Feds do whatever they want with it. If they want to take down a politician, they'll stop at nothing until they have the ammunition. Even if that ammunition means planting evidence they can use later. It's shady. More often than not, the things I get asked to do are things that go against my own personal moral code. So when you say I'm one of the good guys? You have no idea what you're talking about."

"Are you saying you planted evidence?" Emotions whirled. I'd gone from elated that he'd turned his world around to crushed in ten seconds flat.

"No. I said they asked me to. I'm an independent contractor. I take the jobs I want and leave the rest. But the thing is, I don't always know what they're going to do with the information I find. So even when I think I'm working a job I can live with, I never know what the end result will be."

We stood there staring at each other for a long moment. Everything about his stance screamed tension, from his clenched fists, to his hunched shoulders, to the vein pulsing in his neck. But more than that, there was frustration flickering over his chiseled face.

"I love what I do, Scarlett, but I don't love who I do it for," he finally said.

"So don't do it anymore," I said softly and moved in, closing the distance between us.

His gaze flickered to my lips and then settled back on my eyes. "I don't have a choice."

"Of course you do." I reached up and trailed my fingers from his temple to his jawline. "You just said you only take the jobs you want. That it's on your own terms."

"Yeah, but I'm still contracted to work for them. It's part of my sentence."

I stilled. "What does that mean, sentence?"

He stepped back, leaving me cold from his absence. I wrapped my arms around my chest and tried to pretend I hadn't asked the most awkward question of all time.

Devon paced, his sock-clad feet silent on the hardwood floor. "After you left, I sort of lost my mind. I stopped doing jobs and spent all my time trying to figure out where you were. But after months of searching, I came to the conclusion that you were off grid, and the only reason for that was you didn't want to be found."

I nodded. He was right. I'd known he'd come for me, so I emptied my bank account, got on a bus, and then when I landed in Tennessee, I went to work at a temp agency using the identity of one of my former foster siblings.

"Not too long after that I took a job for someone I didn't know. I was reckless. Didn't vet them like I usually did because I needed the cash. It turned out to be a setup. I spent a few months doing time, and then I was offered a deal to work with the Feds instead. The one stipulation—I had to stay clean for five years or I'd have to serve my seven-year sentence in full."

The weight of what he'd said settled over me and I felt my knees go weak. "You broke your probation for me?"

He leveled a stare at me, his expression unreadable. "Yes."

"Why?" The word came out in a whisper.

Devon took two steps, invading my personal space, and cupped my cheek with one hand. "Because it's you."

One lone tear fell down my cheek as I stared up at him, my heart swelling and breaking at the same time. "You know why I left, don't you?"

He nodded. "Because you needed a stable life. One you were never going to get while tied to me."

"But I would've," I choked out and waved a hand around the room. "Look at what you managed to do."

He brushed a lock of my hair behind my ear. "Babe, only because you left. You know the road I was going down. With our backgrounds—my shitty foster parents, their complete disregard for the law and normalcy—it was only going to get worse. If anything, I think I owe you a thank-you."

I shook my head, feeling the crushing weight of my guilt piling down on me. We'd both had hard knocks growing up. Both ended up in the foster system. His foster parents were worse than mine, but neither home had been anything close to stable, or nurturing, or hell, even safe for children. But that didn't mean I could use that as an excuse for what I'd done to him. "Stop. I just left you. Didn't even say good-bye." I pushed away, unable to keep looking him in the eye. "Who does that to someone they love?"

"Scarlett." Devon reached for me, but I took another step back.

"And then I let this happen to me." I waved a hand, indicating my body as if that would explain everything.

He frowned, confusion clear in his expression. "What are you talking about? You look just as gorgeous as you always did."

"Dammit." I spun, turning my back on him. "I let myself be turned. I mated with someone else, Devon. And now I'm alone, a werewolf with no pack."

He was quiet for a moment, and then he stepped around me and gently lifted my chin with two fingers, forcing me to look up at him. "I don't know what happened. And I'd be lying if I said it didn't kill me to know you shared a mate bond with someone other than me. But there's no reason to be ashamed of being a wolf."

"I'm not ashamed of being a wolf," I said as I jerked away. "I'm heartbroken I ended up with someone other than you." The words flew out before I could stop them. Horrified, I slapped my hand over my mouth to keep from incriminating myself further.

"Scarlett—" Devon started, his voice low and full of emotion.

"Stop. I know it's my fault. It's all my fault.

This. Us. You. And I can't change any of it."

He shook his head slowly, and then in one swift movement he gathered me in his arms and bent his head, his lips a fraction of an inch from mine. "If I kiss you now, I'm not going to be able to let you go again, understand?"

I stared at his mouth, unable to process anything except the fact that he still wanted me.

"Scarlett?"

"Yes?"

"Are you ready for this?"

I pressed my hands to his chest and met that intense gaze of his. "Kiss me."

Devon closed the distance, his lips brushing over mine in a silent question, as if he couldn't quite believe this was what I wanted.

But when I clutched his shirt, pulling him to me, his hands slid up my back and his eyes glinted with passion so fierce I could feel his need deep inside my core.

"I said kiss me." Pushing up on my tiptoes, I caught his lower lip between my teeth and sucked gently until he let out a low moan. Then he lifted me up and covered my mouth with his as I wrapped my legs around his waist.

He took two steps, pressing me against the wall, and devoured me with his heated kiss. I melted into him, holding on with everything I had. Emotion burst in my chest, overwhelming me. This was where I was supposed to be. Here in Devon's arms. It was as if no time had passed. The world stopped and all I knew was him.

CHAPTER 7

DEVON

Hunger burst forth in me like I was a starving man. As if I hadn't ever tasted anything as delicious as the pliable woman in my arms. She was mine, not just for the taking, but mine completely. Body and soul. Heart and mind.

And by the way she was matching my searing kiss, I knew without a doubt she felt the same about me.

Breathless, I pulled back slightly and trailed my fingers from her temple down to her neck and across her exposed collarbone. "You're even more beautiful than you were the last time I saw you."

She swallowed, tears standing in her bright blue eyes. "So are you."

I gave her a rueful smile. "Well, I was a punk back then."

"You were my punk." She pressed her hand against my cheek. "I want you so much right now. But I think I owe you an explanation."

I shook my head. "You don't owe me anything, love. I know why you left. Right now I just want to touch you, reacquaint myself with your gorgeous curves, and love you until your cries of pleasure leave your voice husky."

She made a sexy little sound in the back of her throat as her eyes filled with heat.

I felt a self-satisfied smile tug at my lips, and

I bent to run kisses up her neck, only stopping when I reached her ear, and whispered, "I'm dying to be inside you, Scarlett. To feel your slick heat all around me. I want to enter you slowly, savor every inch of you. And then I want to thrust hard and fast until you're screaming my name."

"Oh God," she breathed and tightened her legs around me, pressing her pelvis into my groin. "Yes."

Intense need sparked through me, and the desire to rip off her clothes and take her right there against the wall almost made me come undone. But I couldn't. Not yet. "And then, just before you come, I want you to bite me." I touched that spot on my neck that meets my shoulder. "Make me yours, Scarlett. Bind us together. Forever."

She stiffened and tried to pull away, but she had nowhere to go. I had her trapped against the wall. Shaking her head, she pushed at my chest. "No. Let me down."

I did as she asked but kept my hands flattened against the wall so she couldn't run from me like I knew she wanted to. "Why? I said I wasn't going to be able to let you go again if I kissed you. I even asked if you were ready."

"This is different, Devon. And you know it."

The sound of my given name on her lips didn't feel so foreign anymore. Didn't cut to the quick as it had when I'd heard her say it the night before. "It's not different, love. I want you. All of you."

She cut her gaze away from me and stared at the floor. "You don't know me like this. A lot has happened in five years."

"Yes. It has. But that doesn't matter to me."

She jerked her head up and glared at me in a mix of anger and exasperation. "You can't just decide one day to become a wolf!"

"Why not? Arianna did. She only knew Luc for a few weeks before she decided. I've known you for twenty years. I know you, babe. I've wanted you since I was fourteen years old. And even when you left, I still wanted you. I never stopped. And I'll be damned if I go to bed with you, open myself up to everything that's between us, without knowing where I stand."

Shit.

I stepped back, giving her the space she obviously needed. I'd just laid everything on the table with this woman who'd only been back in my life less than twenty-four hours. Jesus. I was a fucking idiot. But the thought of getting that close to her without knowing she wanted me just as much as I wanted her… I couldn't do it.

Shaking my head, I took a deep breath, steadying myself. "Sorry. I shouldn't have said that. It's too soon. How could you know if you want me as your mate? I—"

Scarlett pressed the tips of her fingers to my mouth, silencing me. "Stop. I do want you as my mate. You're my one and always have been. I would make you mine in an instant if I knew you were ready for it."

Her eyes were big, vulnerable. Almost scared.

My heart stopped for just a moment. She'd said I was hers. I knew then most of the battle was won. Whatever had happened in the past no longer mattered. She wanted me, and one way or another, I'd make sure she got me. I kissed her fingers and then gently pulled her hand away. "I'm fine with being a wolf, and I want you. What else is there to decide?"

"You can't just make this decision on a whim!" She yanked her hand out of mine and paced across the office.

I watched her, my eyes narrowed. There was something else going on with her other than being worried about my choices. She was biting her bottom lip, a sure sign she was nervous. "Scarlett?"

She stopped and turned to stare at me. "What?"

"Just say it. Whatever it is that's on your mind."

She covered her eyes and blew out a long breath. "Can we go in the living room?"

"Sure." I followed her into the next room and sat on my couch as she continued to pace. The familiarity of her actions made it feel like old times. Comfortable. I leaned back and waited.

After a moment, she stopped and turned to face me with her hands on her hips. "The thing is, I never asked to become a wolf."

I stiffened, my entire body on full alert. "You were turned against your will?"

"No, nothing like that."

Frowning, I leaned forward, giving her my full attention. "Then I don't understand."

"Oh, jeez." She started pacing again. "I'm doing this all wrong."

"You're doing fine."

She let out a sad chuckle and shook her head. "No, I'm not fine. How am I supposed to tell you I mated with someone I didn't love?"

A weight I hadn't even known was there lifted off my heart. It was selfish and made me feel like a complete ass, but I couldn't help it. She was mine. The thought of her belonging to anyone else, even for a short time, had all but killed me. "Why then?"

"That doesn't shock you?" Her tone was incredulous.

"No. You must've had a good reason."

Her eyes went soft as all the tension drained from her face. "You're something else."

"Come here," I said and held my hand out.

To my surprise she took it and let me pull her down beside me. I wrapped my arm around her shoulders and pulled her into me just as I had back in the guest room. "Tell me what happened."

This time she didn't hesitate. "I was dating Bax. He was a good guy. Sweet, protective. Law-abiding." She glanced up and gave me a rueful smile.

"Sounds like a catch," I said, careful to keep any irritation out of my tone.

"That's what I kept telling myself even though something was obviously missing. He was fun and good for me, so I stayed in the relationship, even knowing it wasn't going anywhere. Then I was attacked by another wolf. Looking back now, I'm pretty sure my attack had everything to do with Bax and not me personally. They used me to send him a warning of some sort."

She took a deep breath and continued. "The other wolf did considerable damage, and the only way for Bax to save me was to turn me. So when he asked, I agreed. From that day forward we were mates. And while we cared about each other, I don't think either of us ever came close to having what I have with you."

I unconsciously tightened my arm around her, trying to hold her even closer. To keep her safe in my arms. Another wolf had tried to kill her and almost succeeded. "Thank God Bax was around."

She nodded. "Yes. I wouldn't change what he did, but don't you see? I didn't really have a choice. No chance to think about what being a wolf means. I don't want to drag you into this and have you regret it later."

"Scarlett, the only thing I've ever regretted was not listening when you said you couldn't live a life always wondering what would happen if the authorities caught up with me again. I was too far down the rabbit hole and way too cocky. But then you left and I went to jail eight months later. You were right. And now I want my second chance. And I want it forever. I'm clean now. Or was until you walked back in my life." I winked at her. "For me, there's nothing to think about. This craving in my gut? The one that has everything to do with wanting you? It's never eased. I'm yours for the taking."

Her arms tightened around me, and I felt a peace that had been missing since the last time I'd lain with her.

"I love you, Devon," she said, her voice muffled in my shirt.

My heart skipped a beat as I sat there, savoring her words.

She lifted her head and stared me in the eye. "I said I love you."

I smiled and stroked her cheek. "I know. I was just letting it soak in. I love you, too."

We watched each other for a moment, both of us easing into our new reality. Then she uncurled from the couch and held her hand out to me. "I think I'd like to collect on that promise you made me earlier."

"Which one was that?"

"Something about savoring every inch of me…"

"Right." I grinned and leaped up, reaching for her.

She danced away with a laugh and ran up the stairs, me right behind her.

CHAPTER 8
SCARLETT

I STOOD NEXT to Devon's bed near the window, gazing out at the full moon, all the playfulness from the moments before gone. As soon as I'd stepped into the bedroom, the light had called to me, stirred something deep inside me that made me ache for the mate connection.

Turning, I met Devon's smoldering gaze. He was standing in the doorway, watching me, his easy smile replaced by an intensity born of raw sexual need. He wanted me. More than anyone ever had. It sent a bolt of electric heat straight to my core.

I licked my lips and said, "Take your clothes off."

One eyebrow lifted as he swept his gaze down my body in a slow, torturous perusal. "What about you?"

"We'll get to that." My voice was husky, full of rasp.

His eyes flashed with liquid fire as he grabbed a fistful of his T-shirt and pulled it over his head. He wasted no time divesting himself of his jeans, and when he stood gloriously, unabashedly naked before me, he said, "Your turn."

"Lie down." I pointed to the bed, unable to tear my eyes from his rippling abs and well-defined chest, the tattoo so much like mine on his right shoulder. He'd filled out, become a man since the last time I'd had the pleasure of seeing him in the flesh.

He did as I said and propped himself up on a pillow with one hand behind his head.

"Good. That's very good."

His torso was tan as if he spent a lot of time in the sun. Both arms were tattooed from shoulder to wrist, but only one tattoo wrapped around his right calf. Everything about him was gorgeous and made my mouth water. And then, when I spied his shaft, my mouth went dry.

He was so big, so hard. So incredibly hot.

"Touch yourself," I ordered.

"Uh… what?"

"You heard me. Wrap your hand around the base of your cock."

"I'd rather you did that," he said, his voice strained.

I shook my head. "I will, but not yet. I want to see you pleasuring yourself while I strip for you. I want to know that watching me makes you lose control." As a wolf, I was wild. More free than I'd ever been before. I wanted there to be no barriers between us.

When Devon said nothing, I slowly unbuttoned my shirt, letting it hang open just enough to reveal my breasts. And then I slowly ran my fingers down my chest along the edge of the shirt, and with my eyes locked on his, I pushed it open, letting the garment fall soundlessly to the floor.

He sucked in a hard breath, his eyes locked on my breasts as I cupped them and lightly brushed my fingers over my already-taut nipples. "God, Scarlett, you're even more beautiful than I remembered."

"So are you." I ran both hands down my stomach and flicked the button of my jeans open. Then I stopped and stared pointedly at him, waiting.

"Scarlett," he breathed, exasperated, but closed his eyes and moved one hand to hold the base of his hard cock.

"Devon," I breathed.

His eyes reopened, and a slow smile claimed my face as I inched my jeans down, deliberately turning to the side to give him a better view of my backside. Our gazes met and held. Electric currents crackled between us, and all the sex talk and games vanished. All I cared about was touching him, making him *mine*.

I stepped out of the last of my clothing and crawled on my hands and knees up the bed until our lips met in barely a whisper of a kiss.

"I want you more now than I've ever wanted anything." Devon's eyes turned almost silver gray as he threaded his large hand through my long blond hair.

Leaning down, I pressed my lips over his heart and then let myself get lost in the hard lines of his body. He felt so good beneath me, perfect and more turned on than I'd thought humanly possible. The wolf inside me caught the scent of his out-of-control need, and I couldn't hold out any longer.

I had to have him inside me.

Straddling him, I lowered myself and reached for his shaft. But he beat me to it. Still holding himself with one hand, he lifted his hips and pressed his tip against my clit, making me gasp. He ground into me, pleasure nearly driving me insane.

"Oh, Devon. Yes."

He wrapped his other arm around my back and pulled me down, crushing his mouth to mine in an all-possessing kiss. Nipping, sucking, biting. We warred with each other, each of us demanding more.

Devon's hands moved to my hips, grabbing them roughly, his fingers digging into my flesh and lifting me off him.

I let out a little whimper at the loss, but when he pulled me back down, he pressed into my opening, his cock inching into me, just as slow and torturous as he'd promised.

Closing my eyes, I savored his intrusion, reveling in the way he filled me.

"Look at me," Devon said.

My eyes flew open, and my heart nearly shattered into a million pieces at the devastating look of love shining back at me in his silver gaze. Emotion rose up, overwhelming me into breathless silence.

Devon, pulled me all the way down, burying himself deep inside me until we were fully joined, and said, "I waited a long time to be one with you again. I won't let you go this time."

I shook my head, tears stinging my eyes. Blinking them back, I leaned down and whispered, "Mine."

Then with a low growl that came from deep inside my wolf, I started to move.

Devon's hands slid from my hips to cup my ass as he thrust up, meeting my pace. Our movements were slow as we savored each other, but then Devon shifted beneath me and hit just the right spot.

I let out a loud gasp and quickened my

pace, desperate for the delicious friction.

"Yes, babe. You feel amazing," he whispered in my ear.

I moaned in answer.

He chuckled softly, wrapped his arms around my waist, and lifted us both so we were sitting upright. His mouth immediately clamped over my nipple, sucking hard.

Everything pulsed, the wave of ecstasy rolling through me fast and hard. "Oh God," I said, breathless. "Yes. Devon, yes."

He sucked harder, and the tension deep inside me nearly drove me out of my mind. I rocked my hips, desperate for release.

Then suddenly Devon clutched my hips, holding me in place, and roughly thrust up, hitting that perfect spot.

"More!" I cried, arching my back to take

every last bit of him.

But Devon was already thrusting up again, and again, and again, until finally the dam broke and my body shuddered as the orgasm crashed through me.

He held me tight and rained soft kisses over the swell of my breast.

I held still, pulsing around him, luxuriating in the brush of his lips over my skin as I started to recover from the pleasure he'd just given me.

"I could do this forever," he said, flicking his tongue over my breast once more.

"But—Oh!"

He scraped his teeth over the sensitive nub, sending another bolt of heat to all the right places. The intense ache built instantly, and I ground into him, already wanting more of him.

"Devon," I gasped.

He lifted his head, burning desire swimming in his eyes. And then as if some sort of unspoken communication passed between us, we both rolled until Devon was above me. He slipped one arm behind my knee, positioned my leg higher and thrust into me, filling me completely.

We moved together, our pace growing faster and faster with each stroke until Devon grabbed my ass with one hand, holding me tight to him, and ground out, "Make me yours, Scarlett. Now."

The demand in his tone pulled my wolf to the surface. Digging my nails into his back, I jerked my head up and sank my teeth into his shoulder.

He bucked atop me, thrust once, twice, and let out a cry as we both shuddered together.

CHAPTER 9
DEVON

Frantic shouts penetrated my fuzzy consciousness. A dull throbbing pounded at my temples and I rolled over, burying my head into the pillow.

"Devon!" Scarlett's voice filtered through the commotion.

I bolted upright, nausea making my stomach roll. "What is it? What's going on?"

Her arms went around me in a fierce hug. "Thank God you're okay."

I blinked hard, still trying to clear the brain

fog. Then I heard it.

"The computer alarm." I stood abruptly, taking her with me. Someone had gotten past my firewalls.

"I couldn't figure out how to turn it off."

"Forget about that. We have to get out of here." I set her aside and grabbed my jeans, gritting my teeth through the ache in my joints. It was the wolf bite. Everyone experienced it differently, but it wasn't unusual to take a few days for your body to adjust. But I didn't have time to work through it. Someone had infiltrated my system.

Still shoving my feet into my boots, I grabbed her hand and tugged, urging her ahead of me. "Head for the truck. I'll be there in two seconds."

But she didn't move. "I'm not going anywhere without you. Besides, Silas is down there. He'll warn us if someone's coming."

I froze. "Silas is here?"

She nodded. "I'm sorry. I—"

"Jesus, Scarlett. What were you thinking? This is my safe house. No one knew about it. Except you."

"I didn't have a choice." She glared at me, unapologetic. "The alarms on your computer were blaring and I couldn't wake you up. For God's sake, Devon, I was terrified. You've been out for twenty-four hours."

"Fuck. Twenty-four hours?"

She nodded. "It's the bite. Your body was in recovery."

"Right." I ran a hand down my face. No wonder I was a groggy mess. I shook my head, clearing more cobwebs. "Sorry. Dammit! What a shitstorm."

"Agreed." She waved her hand toward the bedroom door. "Get down there and do something about that alarm."

I took off, taking the stairs two at a time as she followed closely behind me. In less than three seconds I was in the office, reaching for the cables to the backup hard drives I kept for such emergencies. Except they were already unplugged and the entire system was down.

I clicked the power button to my mainframe. Nothing.

"I already hit the kill switch," Scarlett said quietly. "I didn't know what else to do. Someone was breaking past all your safeguards."

"You unplugged the hard drives first?"

She nodded, worry swimming in her big blue eyes.

The tightness in my chest loosened a fraction. She might have just saved my ass. I strode over to her and pulled her into a hug. "How long after the alarms started?"

"A minute, maybe two?" She pulled back and met my eyes. "It took me a moment to remember what to do and then to find the switch."

Two minutes. Shit.

If she'd said no more than a minute, I'd be sighing in relief. But two? There were probably half a dozen hackers in the world who could get through my security system. If it was one of them, they could've gotten to my files and traced our location. I stared at the computer, trying to remember what I'd been doing last.

Christ. I'd just gotten done transferring files from the computer I'd hacked, only I hadn't yet logged out. I'd just turned the screen off and had forgotten to shut the program down. What a fucking idiot. I'd left the system vulnerable.

Because I'd been in the FBI mainframe copying files from Bax's partner's computer, that meant more than likely the hacker worked for the FBI. The intruder likely saw my trail and followed it back to me.

We were fucked.

My only hope was that Scarlett had killed the system in time. There was no way to know for sure. I glanced around at all the equipment lining the walls. My hardware. My life's work.

It was all gone. The kill switch had fried it just as it was supposed to.

Footsteps sounded on the hardwood behind me. I tensed, already feeling the echo of the cold steel handcuffs around my wrists. Seven years. The FBI could very well have evidence that I'd broken the terms of my release. They could already be writing my warrant.

Silas appeared in the doorway. "Glad to see you upright, man."

I nodded at him. "Me too. Thanks for keeping an eye on Scarlett."

He chuckled. "It wasn't her I was worried about."

The urge to growl at him was right there beneath the surface, but I swallowed it. My irritation at being hacked wasn't his fault. "We need to get all this out of here. Can you lend me a hand?"

"Sure."

Most of the equipment was useless, but keeping it around would only incriminate me further if any files had been accessed.

It took us less than ten minutes to pile the hardware into the back of my truck. When we were done, I turned to Silas. "Thanks for the help. I'm going to take Scarlett to another safe house. I'll be in touch if we uncover anything useful."

He glanced at the equipment in the back of the truck. "I thought it was trashed."

"It is. But I have backups."

"Right."

Scarlett already had Nate and her bag tucked in my truck. As Silas took off down the dirt road, I ran back in the house, grabbed my essentials, and then set the house alarm to silent. There wasn't anything that I cared about left, but I would be notified if anyone tried to break in or tampered with the alarm. Then I'd know for sure the location had been compromised.

When I hopped in the truck, Scarlett was busy tapping on her phone.

"Who's that?" I asked.

"Silas. He says there's suspicious activity at the end of the road and to take a different route if at all possible."

I cursed under my breath and put the truck in gear.

"Is there another route?" she asked, her eyes wide.

"There is now." I hit the gas and drove off-road, through the trees.

CHAPTER 10

SCARLETT

By the time we emerged from the woods, my teeth were rattling and my butt was numb. The dog had curled up at my feet, apparently unaffected. And just as soon as I was getting used to the flat surface road, Devon took a sharp turn onto another unmarked path.

"Where are we going?" I asked, holding on to the oh-shit handle.

"Slight detour." He pulled into a small clearing and parked next a rusting garbage truck but left the motor running. "Be right back."

Devon leaped out of the truck, and less than a minute later, he'd unloaded all the computer hardware into the back of the garbage truck. When he was done, he slapped his hand on the passenger door and gestured for the driver to take off.

Dust kicked up, obscuring my view as the truck rumbled off onto a rough dirt road.

"Who was that?" I asked him once he was back in the driver's seat.

"Just a contact."

I raised a skeptical eyebrow. "Really? I thought you were on the straight and narrow all this time?"

He glanced over at me, his brow furrowed. "I was."

"And that's why you have a fixer with a

dump truck waiting in the wings?" I'd dismissed the emergency system shutdown on his computer as a holdover from his old life, but this? And why did he have a safe house? He was a hacker for the FBI, not a spy.

He cast me a wary glance. "He's an old contact who happens to live close by."

"And he just happened to be available at a moment's notice?" My chest was getting tight. I'd mated with this man, trusted he'd been honest with me. And now all I could see was the guy I'd left five years ago.

"Yes, Scarlett. He was. Why are you giving me a hard time about this?"

I bit the side of my cheek, not wanting to have this argument right then. But I couldn't seem to hold back. "It just seems awfully convenient is all."

He tightened his grip on the steering wheel. "It does, doesn't it?"

His flippant tone only served to piss me off. "Listen, just because we're mated—"

"Being mated has nothing to do with this." He made a sharp turn down a narrow road that hugged the bayou. "This is about you getting over the past."

I stared at him, incredulous. "Get over the past? How can I when you're up to your old tricks?"

The truck slowed, and then Devon turned to the right, taking us over a rickety old bridge. At the end, he parked the truck behind a row of large cypress trees and killed the engine. He was silent for a long moment before he turned to me. "We need to get a few things straight."

"Yes we do." I crossed my arms over my

chest and dug my fingers into my forearms. "I won't spend my life running from the law."

"Goddammit." He pushed the door open and jumped out of the truck. I sat there watching him, certain he was going to pace like he always did when he was pissed. But instead, he walked over to my side of the truck and held the door open for me.

I frowned.

He answered by holding his hand out to me. Unsure of what else to do, I took it and let him help me out of the truck. Nate climbed up on the seat, watching us.

When I was standing in front of Devon, he brought his hand up and lightly caressed my cheek. "I don't want to fight."

I stiffened and pulled back, not appreciating the way he was avoiding the conversation.

"And I don't want to ignore the elephant in the room."

He sighed and then shrugged. "Fine. You want the truth? I'm not running from the law. Or at least I wouldn't be if you weren't with me. I'd take my chances with my boss. But since there's speculation someone with the Feds is after you, I can't trust anyone except my old crew. Rock, the garbage truck guy? He's really my security tech. He set up everything in my house and is the one who monitors everything. I hired him because he's the best. And he has my back."

Heat crawled up my neck as equal parts shame and relief washed over me. "You burned it all down for me?"

"For us."

Emotion rolled through me. I took a step,

intending to move into his arms, but an alarm went off on Devon's phone, stopping me in my tracks. "Your house?"

He shook his head. "Someone tripped an alarm on the Riveaux property." Glancing down at the phone, he swore.

"What is it?"

"They're here," he said at the exact same time I felt rather than heard the movement of someone just past the trees.

It was then I realized we were *on* the Riveaux property and whoever was out there had come for us.

With his eyes glued to the phone, Devon shoved the keys in my hand. "Go. Take the truck. Send back Silas and the others."

"But—"

"Trust me." Then he lifted his head and

stared me straight in the eye. "And, Scarlett? Hurry."

He took off, disappearing through the trees.

"Son of a... dammit!" I stood there, torn on what to do. My wolf was straining to surface, demanding to shift so she could track her mate. But I pushed her down, determined to do as Devon asked. Everything he'd done so far, he'd done for me.

It took every ounce of will I had, but I climbed into his truck, and with one last look at the trees, I took off back down the road, dialing Silas's number.

I'd just hit the Call button when the driver's side window shattered and a bullet whizzed right past my face. I let out a startled scream as I threw myself across the seat. Nate slid to the floorboard and yelped as he landed in a heap.

A second later, another bullet flew by, this one going straight through the passenger door.

I could not stay there. If I did, I was as good as dead. Weres healed fairly quickly, but if I was hit in a vital area, I'd bleed out for sure back here in the woods. And what if the shooter hit Devon's dog? "Stay down, Nate!" I ordered.

The dog lowered his head, seeming to understand my command.

With the engine still running, I slammed my foot down on the gas pedal. The truck jerked forward as another bullet crashed through the back window.

Holy shit.

Lowering my head until I could barely see out of the windshield, I clutched the steering wheel with a death grip and barreled over the small bridge. I was almost on the paved road when another round of shots was fired, and suddenly the truck lurched, sputtered and died.

I let out a cry of utter frustration, and with pure adrenaline pouring through my veins, I pushed the passenger door open and leaped. The sunny day turned into a world of hazy gray as my bones cracked and elongated, twisted, and shifted, forcing me into my wolf form. I landed easily on all four paws, instinctively heading back the way I came.

Back toward Devon.

CHAPTER 11

DEVON

The message had come in right before the alarm sounded.

They're coming. Meet me at the clearing near marker twelve. Get the girl out of there. ~ Shade

He was a fellow hacker, someone I'd come up the ranks with. I wouldn't have said we were friends. None of us were. But there was a certain amount of professional courtesy between us, and ignoring his message wasn't an option.

I crept through the bayou, keeping an eye out for the flashing red light on my phone. It was the place Shade had asked me to meet him. No doubt he'd set the alarm off on purpose. But why? The thought had barely registered in my brain when I heard the shot come from behind me.

"Scarlett!" I cried and took off back toward the truck, my body straining against my limitations. My muscles bunched and sweat slicked down my face, followed by a roar tearing from the back of my throat. Pain shot through my limbs, and in the next second, everything seized. Bones cracked. My vision blurred. My skin itched.

And then everything cleared and I found myself on all fours, every sense on heightened alert.

I was wolf and my mate was in trouble.

A trace of her faint lily scent filled my senses, and I ran flat out after her. Leaves and branches tugged at my fur, but I paid no attention. There was only one thought on my mind: Scarlett.

Another shot sounded and I let out a howl of distress as I sprinted faster toward her.

Another shot. Then another, followed by a high-pitched yelp.

Blind rage drove me the last few yards through the woods. Then as I burst onto the road, I saw them on the bridge about a football field away. A short, balding man, dressed in camouflage, had his gun pointed at a magnificent blond wolf. Scarlett. I'd know her anywhere.

She lunged and snarled at him, one leg

tucked up against her body. I could smell the copper tang of her blood in the air, but she wasn't letting a leg wound beat her, and she wasn't going down without a fight.

Almost there. A few more feet and I'd rip his fucking arm off.

"You dumb bitch," the shooter jumped back and fired off another shot. Scarlett instinctively flattened her body on the ground, and the bullet whizzed over her head, but before she could get back on her feet, her attacker kicked out, catching her on the side of the head.

I leaped, my teeth bared, and tore into his shoulder.

The shooter screamed and fell backward, taking us both down. I scrambled, coming up on all four paws, but the shooter was one step ahead of me, both hands on his gun, the weapon pointed straight at me.

Scarlett was lying on the road just past him, unmoving, with blood pooling around her.

My heart cracked into a million pieces, and I no longer cared what happened to me. If I lost her right when I'd found her again, nothing would matter anymore.

I hunched my shoulders and snarled, showing my teeth.

His eyes narrowed with cold malice. "Pretty fucking stupid, wolf. You weren't the target, but now that you've interfered I have no choice but to end you."

I felt rather than heard a rustle of leaves behind me.

"What the fuck?" the gunman said, distracted by the movement.

A growl I'd know anywhere came from behind me.

Nate, my golden retriever, was in attack mode.

I didn't hesitate. Just as Nate flew past me, I lunged at the shooter. A hot stinging sensation ripped through my side, but I barely felt it as I sank my teeth into his flesh.

Blood splattered. Someone screamed, but the sound was distant. A ringing started in my head. My vision turned hazy, and the last thing I heard was another shot before everything went dark.

CHAPTER 12

SCARLETT

I WOKE WITH a start, ignoring the pain trying to overpower me. My head ached and a sharp sting pulsed in my hindquarter. The last thing I remembered was a nasty blow to the head. Now all I saw was an empty road.

Devon.

I spun, frantically searching for him and the shooter, but I only found Devon lying unmoving on the road behind me, Nate curled up beside him. Terror rippled through me. There was blood everywhere. Mine. His. And a human's. But the human was gone.

I gingerly made my way to his side, whining as I nudged at his head. He didn't move, but I did hear the faint thump of his heartbeat. Relief washed through me, but it wasn't enough. I needed him. Needed the connection of my mate. And instead of shifting and finding help, my wolf took over and I laid down right next to him, resting my head on his neck.

"Scarlett?"

I jerked my head and growled at the intruder. So did Nate. Anyone who wanted to get to Devon was going to have to go through both of us first.

"Whoa." Fischer, Bax's ex-partner, held up his hands. His jeans were covered in dirt and his normally well-kept appearance was disheveled. "I'm here to help."

I stilled and watched him. What the hell was he doing there?

He nodded toward Devon. "He needs medical attention. If you let me, I can dress his wounds."

I shook my head. No one was touching him.

He gave me a whisper of a smile. "I know you're feeling protective, but you can trust me."

"Can she?" Silas emerged from the trees, a gun strapped to his side. His two brothers Darian and Wren were right behind him. He glanced at me. "Jace sent us when the alarms went off."

"Considering I very likely saved her and her mate's life, I'd say it's a fair assumption," Fischer said.

Silas studied him for a moment. Then he turned to me. "I think you need to shift now."

I hesitated, not wanting to leave Devon, but Silas was right. I needed answers. I nodded once at Silas and then took off running toward the truck. The door was still open, and even though it pained me to do it, I leaped into the cab and shifted back. Thank God we'd thought to pack the car with a bag of clothes, because mine were in shreds from when I shifted. I rummaged around until I found a sundress and hastily pulled it over my head.

Still barefoot, I hopped out of the truck, winced from the burn in my hip where the bullet had grazed me, and went directly to Devon. His wound had stopped bleeding, but the bullet was still lodged in his flesh. Someone was going to have to take that out. Otherwise it would hurt like a bitch when he shifted again.

Before I could ask, Wren knelt beside me,

produced a small leather bag full of medical instruments, and went to work.

"Thank you," I said.

He smiled at me. "It's nothing. You have no idea how many bullets I've extracted."

I raised my eyebrows.

"Military medic."

"Right."

"He's in excellent hands," Silas said.

"That's good. I'd sure hate to explain to my boss that I lost his best agent," Fischer said.

"Agent?" Silas asked and glanced back to Devon.

I ignored the question, not wanting to confirm or deny anything. Turning to Fischer, I asked, "How did you find us?"

"My computer system was hacked. I followed the trail."

Dammit! He knew.

Behind us, Devon let out a low growl.

"Hang on, man. I'm almost done," Wren said. The growling continued for a few moments until Wren let out a sigh of relief. "Got it."

I moved to inspect the damage to my mate.

"It was pretty deep, but he should be okay in a few days. It'll help if you can get him to shift," Wren said.

"I'll try."

Devon was a new wolf, and although he'd already shifted once, it was likely he hadn't had control of it. Not when he thought I was in trouble. And now that he was hurting, getting him to shift back wouldn't be easy.

Kneeling down, I laid one hand on his head and the other on his chest and whispered, "I need you to come back to me."

He stared up at me, his bright blue-gray eyes searching mine.

"You're hurt, but if you shift, you'll start to heal. Trust me."

He closed his eyes and let out a long breath as if to say he didn't have the energy.

"Please, love? I need you. Need to feel your arms around me."

His eyes opened again, and although there was deep-seated weariness there, he got his feet underneath him and, while staring me in the eye, started to shimmer. A moment later, he was kneeling naked in human form.

"Welcome back, Smoke," Silas said.

My mate gave me a tired smile and then called over his shoulder, "It's good to still be here."

I smiled back. "You had me worried."

"So did you."

Wren walked over with a pile of clothes and handed them to Devon. "Here."

"Thanks." Devon wasted no time putting the jeans on, but he gritted his teeth the entire time. And when it came to tugging his shirt over his head, I had to help him. The wound in his torso, while slightly better after the shift, was going to hurt like a bitch for the next twenty-four to forty-eight hours.

Once he was dressed, Silas asked, "Can you drive?"

"I think it's dead," I said, cutting Devon off before he could answer. "A bullet or two killed it."

"No problem. You guys can ride with us." Silas pointed to a black Jeep.

"Why, where are we going?" Devon asked, gritting his teeth through the pain.

"To our cabins. Fischer over here has some explaining to do."

I glanced at him, still unsure if we could trust him. "He knows about the hack," I whispered to Devon.

Devon nodded. "I figured as much." He cast a side-eye glance at the FBI agent. "You gonna report it?"

He shook his head. "No. But if you do it again, I'll have no choice."

"Fair enough." Then he scanned the area. "Where's the shooter?"

Fischer cleared his throat and in a matter-of-fact tone said, "He's been eliminated."

CHAPTER 13

DEVON

We sat at the large wooden table in the main cabin at the bayou resort owned by the Davenne brothers. A pretty human girl named Hannah filled coffee cups and placed trays of eggs, country potatoes, grits, and sausage in the middle of the table.

"Eat up, everyone." She rested her hand on Silas's shoulder as she leaned down to refill his mug. "There's plenty more."

Silas stiffened under her touch, but when he glanced up at her, there was an electric current that sparked between them. "Thank you, Hannah."

"Yes, thank you, Hannah," Wren said, irritation in his tone.

"You're welcome, Wren," she shot back, glaring at him as she retreated from the room.

Wren gave us an apologetic smile. "Sibling issues."

Silas cleared his throat. "Hannah is *his* stepsister, not mine and Darien's. We don't have any issues with her at all."

"That's the problem," Wren mumbled.

I sat back in the chair, enjoying the exchange. Clearly Wren didn't want Hannah anywhere near Silas. I was willing to bet Silas had a very different point of view.

Silas ignored him and turned to Fischer. "Perhaps we could get on with this meeting. I'm sure the agent has better things to do with his time than listen to our family drama."

Fischer took a sip of his coffee and leaned back in his chair. "I don't know. A little family drama sounds better than conspiracy theories and hired guns."

I leaned forward. "Are you saying that gunman was hired to kill Scarlett?"

He nodded. "I've been working on Bax's case for months now. Last week I finally had a breakthrough. I found a piece of evidence that implicated another agent in a human trafficking case. Unfortunately when the agent was indicted, he assumed the information came from Scarlett and he put a hit out on her. By the time we found out, the hit had already been ordered."

"So why not put a detail on her instead of

sending her down here?" Silas asked.

Fischer hesitated.

"I think I deserve to know," Scarlett said quietly.

He met her gaze and nodded. "I think you do, too." Propping his elbows on the table, he leaned forward. "What I'm about to tell you is classified. But since all of you are directly affected, I'm going to fill you in so you can remain vigilant."

"This isn't over," I said.

"You're correct. Although since the shooter has been taken out and the agent in question is incarcerated, we believe the direct threat to Scarlett has been neutralized for now."

I reached over and slipped my hand into Scarlett's, needing to touch her.

"The reason we didn't just give her a detail

is because we believe the agent who's been apprehended isn't the only threat. He had a partner, but we haven't tracked him or her down yet."

"In other words, you can't trust your own, so you're trusting us instead?" Silas asked.

"Exactly. Bax was my partner. I'm certain he was murdered because of his knowledge. I will not let the same thing happen to his mate."

Fierce jealousy exploded deep in my gut at the implication that Scarlett was still mated to Bax. My wolf reared up, and the desire to claim her, to make it known she was mine, was nearly uncontainable. But I forced the urge down, acutely aware we were being warned precisely because of Scarlett's connection to Bax.

"Devon's my mate now," Scarlett said, her eyes flashing. "I appreciate your loyalty to Bax and your help, but if that's the only reason you're here—"

The agent raised his hand, stopping her. "I know. I figured it out back in the bayou. It doesn't matter. Bax would want me to do this, so I am."

"Thank you," I said, meaning it.

"You're welcome."

He took another sip of his coffee, then stood. "That's pretty much all I can say right now. Be alert, and I'll keep you informed if there are any new developments in the case." He threw a few cards on the table. "Please don't hesitate to get in touch if there's any suspicious activity."

Silas stood and shook the agent's hand. "We will. And thanks for the help today."

"Just doing my job." Fischer cut his gaze to

me and Scarlett. "Will you two walk me out?"

Scarlett and I followed the agent out of the house, neither of us saying anything until we got to his black SUV.

"You put the file on my desk back in Nashville, didn't you?" Scarlett asked.

He nodded.

"Why didn't you just tell me?"

"I'd planned to when I dropped it off, but you weren't there. And then I went underground for a few days while running down a lead."

"I see. Well, in that case, thanks for the warning." She gave him a small smile.

"You're welcome." He turned his attention to me. "I assume I can trust you won't be hacking my computer files again?"

"As long as there's no need to."

"Devon!" Scarlett said, admonishing me.

Fischer laughed. "It's quite all right, Scarlett. That's the answer I wanted to hear. No one can be trusted. He's right to be suspicious. But I don't think I have to say what could happen if he's discovered rifling through FBI files."

"I understand," I said. "One thing though."

"Yes?" Fischer raised his eyebrows.

"What happened to Shade?"

The agent grinned. "You're looking at him."

"What?" Thrown completely off guard, I took a step back, pulling Scarlett with me.

He laughed again. "How else did you think I found you?"

"And the hit man? How did he find us?" Scarlett asked.

He shrugged. "I'm not sure. He might have been watching the bar already. Or maybe he followed you from Nashville. All I know is that when I found you two, there he was."

I shook my head in disbelief. "You saved our asses, man. I owe you one."

He shrugged. "Not really. You were doing a pretty good job before I got there. All I did was try to warn you and put him out of his misery. I doubt he was going to survive the wound in his neck."

Scarlett jerked and gave me a questioning glance.

"He was going to shoot you. Nate and I weren't going to stand for that." I cast a glance over my shoulder at my dog sleeping in the shade.

"Well done, then," Scarlett said and put her arm around me.

I held my hand out to Fischer. "Thanks for

the help. It's a pleasure to meet you finally."

"Anytime." He shook my hand and added, "I'm happy to have finally met you as well, Smoke. Keep it clean."

Scarlett and I waited until he disappeared behind the tinted windows of his SUV. Then I bent my head and asked, "You okay?"

She nodded. "You?"

"I will be just as soon as we find a bed."

"To sleep or…?" She grinned.

"Get your mind out of the gutter," I said. "I was talking about sleep."

"Sure you were." Her eyes sparkled as she lifted up on her tiptoes and pressed a light kiss to my lips.

"All right, you win. Sex first, then sleep."

She laughed. "Whatever you say, mate. Whatever you say."

CHAPTER 14

SCARLETT

I STOOD IN the kitchen of Devon's Arts District condo chopping celery. Apparently it was just one of his half dozen homes in and around New Orleans. He'd said it was hiding in plain sight. I said it was living in paradise.

"How's the gumbo coming?" Arianna asked from where she sat at the eat-in bar.

"It's not. Yet. I was told to chop all this." I waved at the pile of vegetables on the counter.

"Are you serious?" She hopped off her stool and came strolling into the kitchen. Without missing a beat, she grabbed a fresh wineglass and filled it with the red wine she'd brought.

"Thirsty?" I asked, eyeing her full glass still sitting on the bar.

She shook her head and pressed it into my hand. "This one's yours."

I smiled and took along sip. Then another. Laughing, I said, "If you get the chef drunk, you never know what you might end up with. Of course, with my track record, it really can't get any worse."

"No chance of that." She grabbed my hand and pulled me into the living room where Devon and Luc were debating the virtues of smart TVs and Nate was snoring on the couch. "Sit. Luc and I will take care of it."

"Sounds good to me," I said and slipped my arm around Devon's waist. "No one really wants me cooking anyway."

Devon glanced down at me. "I love your cooking."

"Right." I rolled my eyes. "You loved the steak I overcooked last night? Or the pasta I undercooked the night before?'

"Enough," Luc said, striding into the kitchen. "I will not be witness to either of you ruining a perfectly good gumbo."

Arianna grinned. "He's so easy."

"I heard that," Luc called from the kitchen.

She winked at us and went to join him.

"Come here." Devon pulled me out onto the balcony. He sat in one of the wood deck chairs and I sat sideways on his lap.

There was joy in his gaze I wasn't used to seeing. Every day over the past few weeks, his light had been shining brighter, as if he was really living for the first time ever. "You're gorgeous," I murmured and pressed a kiss along his jawline.

"And you're sexy as hell." He inched his hand up my skirt and along my thigh, brushing his fingers over the edge of my silk lace panties.

I knew I should say something, swat his hand away, but I didn't want to. We had five years to make up for, and I cherished every touch, every kiss, every new discovery.

Devon used his other hand to brush a lock of hair from my eyes. "I wanted to tell you something."

"Oh, yeah? What's that?"

"Well, maybe not tell you so much as ask you."

I tilted my head, waiting.

He cleared his throat. "I know we've only

been back together for a few weeks, but I wanted you to know that ever since you've come back into my life, I've been… different."

"Different?" His odd tone was making me nervous.

He nodded. "Less intense."

"Okay."

"Before you came back, I spent all my time holed up in my office working."

That wasn't news. That was the way he'd been before too. Even though he'd barely spent any time with his computers lately, I just assumed we were in a honeymoon phase, spending most of our time lounging in bed. "I never expected you to give up your work," I said, my tone soft. "I know it's in your blood. I don't want to change you, Dev."

He chuckled. "That's just it. You already

have. Or *we* have. I don't know if it has anything to do with me turning wolf or if it's because I have you, but I no longer feel that restless drive I used to. Before, it was almost an addiction. Now, although the challenge still excites me, I'm not driven like I used to be."

"Is that a good thing?" I held my breath, waiting for his answer.

"Yes, love. It's a good thing."

I wrapped my arms around his neck and smiled. "You have no idea how happy that makes me."

He covered my hand with his and started to stroke my fingers. When he got to my ring finger he paused, took a deep breath, and asked, "Happy enough to marry me?"

I stiffened as shock slammed into me. Then I sat up straight and stared him in the eye.

"What did you just say?"

He held a large princess-cut diamond up. "Scarlett, will you marry me?"

My breath caught and my heart started to pound against my rib cage. "Are you… serious?"

Smiling, he slipped the ring onto my finger and kissed my knuckles. "Very."

"Holy shit." I lifted my hand and stared at the shimmering diamond.

"I want a family, Scarlett. You know I've never really had one, aside from Arianna. And I want to start one with you. I always have."

Tears sprang to my eyes. God, I wanted that more than anything, too. And he knew it. "But we can't start a family… not right now. At least not until this mess with the FBI is over."

One tear fell and he gently wiped it away.

"Babe, I'm in no hurry. All I want is to marry you and know that one day we'll have little ones terrorizing us."

Whatever it was that was holding me back vanished, and I let out a small giddy laugh as I said, "Yes. Absolutely yes. I'll marry you."

"Thank God." Devon tightened his arms around me, and crushed his lips to mine, showing me exactly just how much my saying yes meant to him.

I sank into the kiss, matching his fervor with my own. When we finally came up for air, we were both winded and grinning like fools.

Through the glass I spotted Arianna and Luc giving us the thumbs-up as Arianna danced around, deliriously happy.

"I think we better go celebrate before Arianna bursts something," Devon said.

"I have a question first," I said, my voice teasing.

"Oh? What's that?"

"About that family you wanted?"

He gave me a curious look. "Yes?"

"I think we're going to need a lot of practice in the baby-making department. When do you think we can get on that?"

His lips turned up into a sexy half smile as he stood, still holding me in his arms. "Just as soon as I can throw my sister out. Give me five minutes."

"Hmm, that sounds interesting. But who's going to make the gumbo?"

"We'll get takeout."

I threw my head back and laughed. "That's the perfect answer."

Sign up for Kenzie's newsletter at www.kenziecox.com to be notified of new releases. Do you prefer text messages? Sign up for text alerts! Just text SHIFTERSROCK to 24587 to register.

Book List:

Wolves of the Rising Sun

Jace

Aiden

Luc

Craved

Silas

Darien

Wren